Miss McKenzie Had a Farm

Written by Tim Johnson
Illustrated by Linda Kelen

STECK-VAUGHN®
C O M P A N Y

A Division of Harcourt Brace & Company

www.steck-vaughn.com

Miss McKenzie had a farm.

On her farm, she had Cow, Goat, and Chicken.

Cow and Goat liked to work.

Chicken liked to sing.

Miss McKenzie looked at the calendar.

Miss McKenzie said, "Oh no, it is the first of June."

Cow said, "Oh no, it is the first of June."

Goat said, "Oh no, it is the first of June."

Chicken said, "Oh yes, I will sing a tune."

Miss McKenzie said, "Oh no, the rent is due!"

Cow said, "Oh no, the rent is due!"

Goat said, "Oh no, the rent is due!"

Chicken said, "Oh yes, I can sing ♪♫ **Happy Birthday to You.**♪"

4

Miss McKenzie looked in her purse
and said, "Oh no, I cannot pay."

Cow said, "Oh no, I cannot pay."

Goat said, "Oh no, I cannot pay."

Chicken said, "Oh yes, I can sing
♫ **Down by the Bay.**" ♪

5

Miss McKenzie said, "We must make some money, Cow and Goat."

Cow said, "We must make some money, Cow and Goat."

Goat said, "We must make some money, Cow and Goat."

Chicken said, "Oh yes, I can sing Row, Row, Row Your Boat."

Miss McKenzie said, "How can we do it?
Let's think of a way."

Cow said, "Let's think of a way."

Goat said, "Let's think of a way."

Chicken said, "I can sing
Polly-Wolly Doodle All the Day."

Miss McKenzie said, "I have an idea.
We'll need good luck."

Cow said, "We'll need good luck."

Goat said, "We'll need good luck."

Chicken said, "Yes, I can sing
 ♪ **Five Little Ducks.**"♪

Miss McKenzie said, "Let's build
a farm stand."

Cow said, "Let's build a farm stand."

Goat said, "Let's build a farm stand."

Chicken said, "Yes, my songs are grand."

9

Miss McKenzie said, "We'll need paint and wood."

Cow said, "We'll need paint and wood."

Goat said, "We'll need paint and wood."

Chicken said, "Of course, I'll sing for the neighborhood."

Miss McKenzie said, "We need to make a big sign."

Cow said, "We need to make a big sign."

Goat said, "We need to make a big sign."

Chicken said, "Sure, my songs are fine."

Miss McKenzie said, "It's good that we like farming."

Cow said, "It's good that we like farming."

Goat said, "It's good that we like farming."

Chicken said, "Of course, I can be charming."

Miss McKenzie said, "Now we're open and ready to go!"

Cow said, "Now we're open and ready to go!"

Goat said, "Now we're open and ready to go!"

Chicken said, "On with the show!"

13

Miss McKenzie said, "This is hard work. Now we have a chance."

Cow said, "Now we have a chance."

Goat said, "Now we have a chance."

Chicken said, "Of course, I can sing and dance."

Miss McKenzie said, "We sold everything."

Cow said, "We sold everything."

Goat said, "We sold everything."

Chicken said, "I can draw my picture
while I sing."

Miss McKenzie said, "Now we can pay
the rent. Let's take a rest!"

Cow said, "Let's take a rest!"

Goat said, "Let's take a rest!"

Chicken said, "Thank you. Thank you.
I was the best!"